OUTLAW

Laura Shenton

OUTLAW

Laura Shenton

Iridescent Toad Publishing

Iridescent Toad Publishing.

Cover by Kuro Ishi Arts.

First edition. ISBN 978-1-913779-25-2

Chapter One

Lilyana's wings twitched nervously as she walked towards the market stall. The pink membranes caught the golden light of the late afternoon sun filtering through the dense, woven canopy of Merchant's Square, casting a soft rose-coloured glow on the weathered cobblestones beneath her feet. She kept her wings close to her back – a habit most fae had developed after generations of living under vampire rule. It was a survival instinct, passed down from parent to child. Drawing attention to oneself was dangerous, especially in the more affluent districts of Grindmore where vampire nobility frequently prowled, their alabaster faces impassive as they surveyed what they considered their rightful domain.

The marketplace hummed with subdued activity – fae merchants and customers alike conducting their business in hushed tones, everyone moving with the careful precision of prey animals in open territory. The scent of spices, overripe fruit, and the underlying funk of too many bodies in too small a space hung in the air. Lilyana brushed past a stall selling glass charms, careful not to disturb the dangling trinkets that would announce her passing with their delicate chimes.

"Three pallberries, please," she said, placing a few copper coins on the wooden counter, their metal dull from countless exchanges. She avoided eye contact with the elderly fae merchant, another survival instinct learnt early in life.

The old woman's gnarled fingers trembled as she gathered the luminescent blue fruits, their skin nearly translucent, revealing the pulsing glow within. Her hands bore the calluses and scars of a lifetime of labour, her fingernails stained blue from handling the precious berries. "Taking care of someone sick?" she whispered, leaning forward to address Lilyana, her own moth-like wings – tattered from age and hardship – fluttering slightly against her hunched back.

Lilyana nodded, her silver facial markings catching the light. "My neighbour's son. The fever hasn't broken for three days." She swallowed, remembering the child's burning forehead, his pitiful whimpers as his wings twitched with each laboured breath. "His mother is beside herself with worry."

Pallberries were one of the few natural remedies that worked on fae illnesses. Their healing properties were well-known, their juice capable of reducing fever and fighting infection when nothing else would work. While not illegal for fae to possess, they were heavily taxed – another way the vampire aristocracy maintained control over the fae population, turning even medicine into a tool of oppression.

The merchant's wrinkled face softened momentarily with compassion. "I'll add an extra one," she murmured. "For the child." Her kindness – a small resistance against the crushing system they lived under – brought a lump to Lilyana's throat.

As the merchant's hand extended to drop the fruit into Lilyana's palm, her fingers curling protectively around the precious cargo, a shadow fell across the stall. The temperature seemed to drop several degrees instantly. A hush fell over the nearest stalls, conversations dying mid-sentence.

"Well, well. What do we have here?"

The voice slid over Lilyana like ice water, raising goosebumps along her arms and making the delicate membranes of her wings contract involuntarily. She didn't need to turn around to know its owner was a vampire. The merchant's face had drained of all colour, her wings now completely still – a prey response in the presence of a predator, an evolutionary instinct that even centuries of coexistence had failed to eliminate.

Lilyana slowly turned to face the voice, her heart hammering so loudly she was certain everyone could hear it. A tall, elegantly dressed vampire stood before her, his pale features arranged in an expression of exaggerated curiosity. His eyes were the colour of burnished copper, gleaming with malicious intelligence. He wore an immaculate charcoal suit with a deep crimson waistcoat, the fabric finer than anything a fae would possess in their lifetime.

Two enforcement officers flanked him, their black uniforms bearing the silver emblem of Grindmore Security Force, their hands resting casually on the hilts of their shock batons.

"Just purchasing some fruit, sir," Lilyana said, lowering her gaze respectfully, though every instinct in her body screamed at her to run. She could feel the weight of dozens of eyes on her, other fae watching from the peripheral shadows, simultaneously grateful and guilty that they weren't the ones being singled out.

"Is that so?" The vampire, clearly a nobleman by his attire and the ornate silver pin designating him as a member of one of the ruling houses, circled her slowly, his footsteps deliberate and measured on the cobblestones. He moved with the liquid grace of a predator, unhurried because his prey had nowhere to escape. "Strange choice, pallberries. Especially considering the new regulation."

Lilyana's heart stopped, her breath catching painfully in her throat. A cold dread settled in her stomach, heavy as lead. "What new regulation, sir?" Her voice remained steady, a minor victory, though her wings gave an involuntary twitch that betrayed her anxiety. The pallberries felt suddenly hot in her palm, like tiny coals burning against her skin.

The nobleman's smile widened, revealing the tips of his fangs, sharp and white against the bloodless pale of his lips. "As of this morning, all pallberry sales must be registered with the Health Ministry. Didn't you see the proclamation?" He pointed to a notice board across the square – one that Lilyana was certain hadn't been there earlier. "The penalty for unregistered transactions is quite severe. For both parties involved." His gaze flickered meaningfully to the old merchant, who seemed to shrink further into herself.

"I... I didn't know," Lilyana said desperately, her mind racing through escape options, each as impossible as the last. This was how they worked – new arbitrary rules implemented without warning, designed to catch fae in technical violations, giving the vampires legitimate-seeming reasons for arrests and punishments. A system designed to maintain fear, to remind the fae that safety was always conditional, freedom always an illusion. "I can register the purchase now if…"

"It's too late for that, I'm afraid," the vampire said, feigning regret with a theatrical sigh that fooled no one. His copper eyes gleamed with the pleasure of a cat that had cornered a mouse. "Officers, this one needs re-education." He plucked one of the pallberries from her hand and crushed it between his fingers, watching with satisfaction as the blue juice dripped onto the ground, its healing glow sputtering and dying as it hit the cold stone. "Grindmore Prison Academy will help her learn to pay better attention to proclamations."

The mention of the academy sent a ripple of fear through the gathered onlookers. Someone gasped. A mother pulled her child closer, her wings curling protectively around his small form.

"No, please," Lilyana protested, feeling panic rise in her chest. Her wings began to beat frantically, an autonomic response she couldn't control. "I didn't know about the new rule. No one told us."

The nobleman raised an eyebrow, the picture of affronted authority. "Arguing with a superior? Add insubordination to her charges." He brushed an invisible speck of dust from his immaculate sleeve, as if the very act of speaking to her had somehow contaminated him. "Perhaps extended re-education is in order."

The enforcement officers moved forward in unison, their expressions impassive, their faces trained to show nothing – no pity, no anger, no humanity. One produced a pair of wing-binders – a cruel device designed to painfully compress a fae's wings against their back, the metal bands etched with runes to dampen their natural glow.

"This isn't right," Lilyana said, backing away, her heel catching on a loose cobblestone. She stumbled slightly, adrenaline surging through her veins. "I've done nothing wrong. How can you enforce a rule no one knows about?" Her voice rose slightly, drawing disapproving glances from other fae who knew better than to question authority.

"You've broken the law," one officer stated flatly, his voice mechanical, rehearsed. "And now you resist arrest. That's another violation."

The other officer circled behind her, the heels of his boots clicking against the cobblestones with precise, measured steps. Lilyana knew that if she tried to fly, they would see it as another violation – an abundance of violations could result in wing-clipping as punishment. The thought sent ice through her veins, a terror uniquely horrifying to any fae. Wings weren't just for flight; they were connected to a fae's life force, their essence. Clipping was more than physical mutilation – it was spiritual amputation.

"Fine," she said, holding her wrists out, her wings drooping in defeat. The remaining pallberries fell from her hand, rolling across the cobblestones, their precious healing power wasted. "But I want it noted that I was unaware of any new regulation."

The officer in front of her laughed, a harsh sound devoid of humour, as he snapped cold metal shackles around her wrists. They bit into her skin, unnecessarily tight, a small cruelty that was just the beginning. "Noted," he said mockingly, his breath smelling of stale blood. "I'm sure someone at the academy will take that into account during your orientation."

As they forced the wing-binders onto her, the metal bands constricting around the delicate membranes, causing sharp pain to radiate across her back and into her shoulder blades, Lilyana caught sight of the nobleman helping himself to fruit from the merchant's stall without paying. He selected the ripest specimens, examining each one with exaggerated care before pocketing them, while the old woman stood frozen, eyes downcast. She didn't dare protest – they both knew the cost of such defiance.

This was Grindmore – a city of shadows and whispers, of arbitrary rules and cruel enforcement, where vampires held absolute power and fae existed merely at their mercy, their lives as fragile as candle flames in a storm. And now Lilyana was headed to the most feared place in the territory: Grindmore Prison Academy, where "re-education" was just another word for torture, where fae went in whole and came out broken – if they came out at all.

As they marched her through the square, Lilyana's mind raced with thoughts of escape, each more desperate and impossible than the last. She caught glimpses of other fae averting their eyes, unwilling to witness her shame lest they be next. Some made furtive protective gestures, ancient signs of warding that offered no real protection but provided the illusion of doing something in the face of helplessness. The dampened pink glow from her wings reflected off the pavement as tears threatened to fall. She blinked them back fiercely, refusing to give her captors the satisfaction of seeing her break before she even reached the academy gates.

The prison transport was waiting at the edge of the market – a black carriage with barred windows and the ominous seal of the academy emblazoned on its side, the paint gleaming wetly in the fading light of early evening. The two black horses at the front stood unnaturally still, their eyes clouded white – reanimated beasts that needed neither food nor rest. Through the bars, Lilyana could make out other fae prisoners, their wings bound like hers, their eyes hollow with fear and resignation. Some bore bruises, others had the vacant stare of those who had already retreated into themselves, finding what meagre protection they could in dissociation.

One of the officers shoved her roughly towards the carriage door, his hand lingering inappropriately at the small of her back where her wings joined her body, a particularly sensitive area for fae. Lilyana stumbled into the darkened interior of the carriage, finding a small space on a bench between two other prisoners. The air inside was stifling. The door slammed shut with a final-sounding clang, and the carriage lurched forward, its wheels grinding against the cobblestones.

"First time?" whispered a fae next to her, his wings a dull orange, the membranes torn in places and compressed in a painful position by the binders. His face was gaunt, his cheekbones sharp beneath his skin, but his eyes still held a spark of defiance.

Lilyana nodded, not trusting her voice to remain steady if she spoke. Her wrists chafed against the metal shackles, and each bump in the road sent fresh pain through her confined wings.

"Don't show fear," he advised, his voice barely audible over the rumble of the carriage wheels and the occasional sob from another prisoner. "That's what they feed on – your terror. It's like ambrosia to them." He shifted slightly, wincing as the movement pulled at his bound wings. "And whatever you do, protect your wings at all costs. They know what they mean to us. It's the first thing they'll threaten."

Lilyana touched the hexagonal silver markings along her jawline – a decoration her mother had given her nearly six years ago, on her eighteenth birthday, symbols of her family history that she would carry forever. The smooth, familiar patterns under her fingertips brought a momentary comfort, a connection to something beyond this nightmare. "How long will they keep us?"

The man laughed bitterly, the sound hollow and broken. "Until they decide you're "educated". Could be weeks. Could be years. Some never leave." He fell silent as a guard rapped sharply on the partition separating the prisoners from the driver, the sound like a gunshot in the confined space.

The carriage wound its way through the narrow streets of Grindmore, the wheels clattering over increasingly uneven ground, jostling the prisoners against each other. Gradually, they left the city centre behind, the buildings growing more sparse, the streets wider and less maintained. Through the barred windows, Lilyana watched as the urban landscape gave way to the twisted, leafless trees that populated the outskirts of the city, their gnarled branches reaching towards the darkening twilight sky. In the distance, a massive structure gradually came into view – a gothic monstrosity of black stone and twisted spires.

Grindmore Prison Academy.

The sight of it made Lilyana's stomach clench with dread. Stories of what happened behind those walls circulated among fae communities in whispers – tales of endless darkness, of screams that echoed through stone corridors, of fae who returned with their wings permanently damaged, their spirits broken beyond repair. Some said the vampires fed on the prisoners, not just their blood but their fear and pain, harvesting emotions like farmers harvested crops.

Lilyana's wings ached against their bindings as the carriage approached the main gates – massive iron bars flanked by watchtowers manned by vampire guards, their silhouettes sharp against the grey sky. Gargoyles perched along the outer wall, their stone faces contorted in expressions of malice. As the gates creaked open with an ominous groan of metal, Lilyana had the distinct feeling that she was being swallowed whole by some ancient, malevolent beast.

The orange-winged fae beside her seemed to sense her mounting panic. "Remember," he whispered as the carriage rolled to a stop in the courtyard, gravel crunching beneath the wheels. "No matter what they do to you, don't let them break your spirit. That's what they really want. More than your blood, more than your labour – they want your surrender."

Guards approached the carriage, their movements synchronised, emotionless. The door was flung open, allowing a gust of cold air to rush in, carrying with it the smell of damp stone and something else – something metallic and sickly-sweet that Lilyana recognised instinctively as old blood.

As rough hands dragged her into the gathering darkness of Grindmore Prison Academy, the massive doors swinging shut behind her with the finality of a tomb being sealed, Lilyana made a silent promise to herself. She would endure. She would survive. And somehow, someday, she would escape this place.

Chapter Two

The processing room stank of fear and antiseptic – a nauseating combination that clung to the walls and seemed to seep into Lilyana's pores. She stood in line with a dozen other new arrivals, all fae with wings bound painfully behind their backs. The bindings cut into the delicate membrane where wing met shoulder, sending constant waves of sharp discomfort through her body with each breath. Her wrists were bare now – the guards had stripped the prisoners of their shackles upon entry, a small mercy that did nothing to ease the oppressive atmosphere.

Guards – all vampires – patrolled the edges of the room, their pale faces expressionless save for the occasional curl of lip or narrowing of eyes. Their emotions ranged from bored indifference to sadistic anticipation, evident in the way some fingered their weapons or let their gaze linger too long on the more vulnerable-looking prisoners. Their boots clicked against the cold stone floor in a rhythm that seemed designed to fray already frazzled nerves.

"Strip," barked a female vampire officer, her fangs glinting under the harsh fluorescent lights that buzzed overhead like angry insects. She wore her dark hair pulled back in a severe bun, emphasising the sharp angles of her face. Her uniform – black with silver insignia – was immaculate, as if even a speck of dust wouldn't dare cling to her. "Everything off, now. No exceptions, no delays."

Lilyana hesitated, her fingers hovering at the hem of her shirt. The room's chill raised goosebumps on her exposed arms. She glanced at the others who had already begun removing their clothes, their movements awkward due to the wing-binders. Some kept their eyes downcast in shame; others stared blankly ahead, already retreating into the recesses of their minds – a survival tactic Lilyana would soon come to understand.

"Did I stutter?" The officer approached with deliberate slowness, each step a threat. She twirled a shock baton casually between long-fingered hands, the weapon's electric tip occasionally sparking blue. Her eyes – unnaturally bright against her pale skin – locked onto Lilyana's with predatory focus. "Or would you perhaps prefer I help you? I assure you, my methods are far less gentle."

With trembling fingers, Lilyana began to undress, the simple task made difficult by her bound wings and the eyes that watched her every move. The humiliation burned hot on her cheeks, spreading down her neck in blotchy patches of colour that only seemed to amuse the guards further. She focused on a spot on the wall – a small crack in the otherwise featureless grey surface – and counted each breath, determined not to break, adamant not to give them the satisfaction of seeing her crumble.

"Faster!" the officer snapped, striking the floor near Lilyana's feet with the baton. The electric crack echoed through the room, followed by the acrid smell of ozone. Everyone jumped, several fae whimpering involuntarily. "We haven't got all day, and there are many more of you vermin to process."

The naked prisoners were led one by one through a decontamination shower – a narrow metal stall with nozzles on all sides that shot icy water mixed with chemicals that made Lilyana's skin burn and her eyes water. The liquid had a strange, metallic taste when it inevitably got into her mouth, making her gag and spit. It seemed designed for discomfort rather than cleanliness, another small cruelty in a place built on suffering.

The shower guard – a burly male vampire with a shaved head and a network of scars across his throat – took particular pleasure in directing the high-pressure spray at the prisoners' bound wings. His massive hands adjusted the controls with surprising dexterity, increasing the pressure whenever someone seemed to be adjusting to the discomfort. Several fae cried out in pain as the powerful jets hit the sensitive membranes of their wings, the sound echoing off the tiled walls.

"Fragile little butterflies, aren't you?" He laughed, the sound deep and hollow, devoid of real humour. He deliberately targeted the sensitive joint where Lilyana's wings connected to her shoulder blades, watching with interest as she bit her lip to keep from crying out. "Not so magical now, are you? Just wet, pathetic creatures at our mercy."

Once the shower was over, it was time for inspection – a degrading process where each prisoner was examined for contraband and catalogued for the prison records. Lilyana stood dripping and shivering on a cold metal platform as a vampire physician impassively documented her physical characteristics. The room was deliberately kept cold, she realised – another small torment. Water pooled at her feet, mixed with the occasional drop of blood where the wing-binders had cut into her skin. Even with them now removed, the ache lingered – a dull, pulsing reminder of their cruel restraint.

"Pink wings, unusual," the doctor noted in a clinical tone, tapping the observation into a tablet. He circled her like she was a specimen, refusing to acknowledge her humanity. His white coat was pristine, contrasting with the stained walls and floors around them. "Silver facial markings along the jaw, cheekbones and abdomen – consistent with southern fae bloodlines. Luminous pink eyes – rare genetic variation. Height: five feet, four inches. Weight: approximately one hundred and twenty pounds. No obvious deformities or illnesses."

He pressed a button, and a camera flashed from multiple angles, capturing her humiliation for the prison files. Heat prickled at her cheeks, but she kept her head high, swallowing the bitterness rising in her throat.

The doctor paused, examining her wings with clinical detachment. "Wing span approximately fourteen feet when extended. Slight discolouration at the tips – early signs of stress response." He made another note. "Subject seems physically adequate for standard labour assignments."

Finally, prison uniforms were distributed – a coarse black jumper and trousers that scratched against her skin, the fabric stiff with industrial detergent and too many washings. The material was deliberately rough, Lilyana suspected, another small misery to remind them of their place. Even without the wing-binders, she felt just as trapped.

The new prisoners were marched through a series of heavy metal doors, each clanging shut behind them with finality, the sound reverberating through Lilyana's chest. Each door was heavier than the last, each corridor narrower and more oppressive. They descended deeper into the facility via a spiralling ramp, the temperature dropping with each level. The air grew denser, carrying the smell of damp stone and distant mould. Lilyana realised they were moving underground, away from any possibility of natural light, away from the sky that was the birthright of all fae.

The lighting became increasingly sparse as they descended, with long stretches of near darkness between pools of harsh artificial light. For creatures born to sunlight and open skies, this descent into the earth felt like a violation of their very nature. Several of the fae began to tremble, not from cold but from a primal fear taking hold.

The cell block, when they finally reached it, was a vast open space with three tiers of cells lining the walls. Metal walkways connected the upper levels, and guard stations were positioned at strategic points throughout. The lighting was dim, barely enough to see by, the shadows thick and almost tangible. This was less of a problem for Lilyana with her luminous eyes, but she could see other fae squinting and stumbling, already disorientated. The air was stagnant, carrying the echoes of distant cries and the occasional metallic clang of doors or the electronic crackle of shock batons being activated.

Rows of cells stretched into the distance, most closed but some open, revealing glimpses of the lives contained within – small, desperate spaces made personal only by the minimal possessions allowed. Above them, catwalks allowed guards to patrol and observe, their footsteps creating a constant, irregular drumbeat that formed the heartbeat of the prison.

"Welcome to your new home," announced their escort, a tall vampire with a captain's insignia on his immaculate uniform. His voice carried easily in the open space, bouncing off the stone walls. His pale features were handsome in the way of all vampires, but his eyes held no warmth, only a calculating intelligence that seemed to assess the prisoners' worth as resources rather than beings. "This is C Block. You'll learn the rules quickly, or you'll suffer the consequences just as swiftly." He smiled thinly, revealing just a hint of fang. "Remember, your comfort – indeed, your very existence – is entirely at our discretion."

Beside Lilyana, a female fae trembled, her breath coming in shallow, uneven gasps. Lilyana could feel the tension radiating from her, the way her wings twitched instinctively as if yearning for escape. Nearby, another fae's fingers were curled so tightly into fists that his knuckles had turned white.

Their escort gestured to the cells around them. "These will be your quarters. Two or three to a cell, depending on population numbers. You will rise at the morning bell, work your assigned shifts, eat at designated times, and return to your cells for lockdown. Any deviation from this schedule will result in immediate disciplinary action."

One by one, prisoners were assigned to cells, their names called out in alphabetical order, each name echoing through the cavernous space. Lilyana watched as her fellow new arrivals were led away, some trembling, others walking with forced dignity. She tried to memorise faces, to forge some connection with these companions in misery, but they were all taken away too quickly.

"Lilyana Moondrop," a guard called, consulting a digital tablet. "Cell C seventeen, second tier."

Lilyana was directed to follow a different guard, a compact vampire with close-cropped hair and an expression of perpetual disgust. They climbed a metal staircase to the second level, their footsteps ringing out against the grated steps. The walkway was narrow, with only a simple railing separating them from a twenty-foot drop to the concrete floor below.

The guard unlocked the heavy door of C seventeen with a keycard, then punched a code into a keypad beside it. The door slid open with a hydraulic hiss, revealing a space barely large enough for the bunks it contained. The guard gestured for her to enter, his lips curling in what might have been intended as a smile but looked more like a grimace.

"Fresh meat for you two," he called into the darkness, his voice carrying a note of cruel amusement. "Play nice. Or don't – entertainment's hard to come by down here."

The door closed behind her, followed by the electronic beep of the lock engaging. Lilyana stood perfectly still, allowing her eyes to adjust to the even dimmer light inside the cell. A small, barred window in the door allowed a weak beam of light from the corridor to filter through.

Lilyana could make out two figures sitting on bottom bunks on opposite sides of the small space. Neither moved immediately, assessing her as she assessed them. The air in the cell was thick with tension and the lingering tang of body odour.

"Well, well, what have we here?" The voice came from her left – a female fae with striking blue wings. She stood, approaching Lilyana with a critical eye, circling her slowly and carrying herself with an air of defiance, her posture straight, her chin tilted upward.

"Pink wings. How precious. And those silver markings – southern bloodline, aren't you? Probably never even had to fly above a thunderstorm to survive."

"Back off, Soren," said the other occupant – a female fae with pale yellow wings veined with gold. A long scar cut across one cheek, pulling her features slightly askew and giving her a perpetually wary expression. She remained seated on her bunk but watched the interaction carefully. "She's had enough for one day. We all remember our first day here."

"Just saying hello," Soren replied, completing her circle around Lilyana before stopping directly in front of her. Up close, Lilyana could see the small, intricate tattoos around Soren's eyes – status markers from one of the northern fae clans, known for their warrior traditions. "I'm Soren. That's Vidia. And this..." She gestured around the tiny cell, her movement encompassing the stained walls, the thin mattresses, and the single small sink and toilet in the corner. "...is hell. Or as close as the vampires could design it for our kind."

"I'm Lilyana," she said as she straightened her shoulders.

"What are you in for?" Vidia asked, her voice gentler than Soren's, with a melodic quality that suggested she might have been a singer before imprisonment. She shifted on her bunk, making room as if inviting Lilyana to sit, though she didn't explicitly offer.

"Buying pallberries without proper registration," Lilyana replied, the absurdity of her situation hitting her anew. The words sounded hollow even to her own ears – such a minor infraction to result in such severe punishment.

Soren laughed bitterly, the sound bouncing off the close walls. "That's a new one. Pallberries. Criminally dangerous fruit, clearly." Her sarcasm was thick enough to cut. "I'm here for "disrupting the peace". I was caught walking the hills during the small hours. A passing vampire patrol decided it was "incitement to rebellion"."

"And I," Vidia said quietly, her fingers absently tracing the scar on her cheek, "refused a vampire's advances. When I said no, he tried to take what he wanted anyway. I defended myself – kicked him where it hurt. The next day, guards came to my home, claiming I had "assaulted a citizen of the upper class"."

Lilyana felt a chill run through her that had nothing to do with the cold cell. The unjust nature of their imprisonment confirmed what she had always suspected: it was about control, about reminding the fae of their place in the hierarchy, about crushing any spark of defiance before it could grow into a flame.

"Top bunk's yours," Vidia pointed to the empty bed above her own. The metal frame looked flimsy, the thin mattress sagging in the middle. "There's a blanket. It's not much, but it's something. If you're lucky, there aren't too many bugs in it."

Lilyana climbed awkwardly onto the bunk. The thin mattress offered little comfort, and the single coarse blanket – grey with age and countless washings – did little to ward off the chill that seemed to emanate from the very walls.

From her new vantage point, she could see more of the cell – the small shelf built into the wall that held a few meagre possessions, the crude drawings scratched into the wall beside Soren's bunk, the tiny mirror above the sink that was made of polished metal rather than glass. And everywhere, signs of the prisoners who had come before her – initials carved into the bed frame, mysterious stains on the walls, and most disturbingly, the ceiling above her where previous occupants had scratched markings – tallies, she realised with a sinking heart, counting days.

"How long have you both been here?" she asked, unable to tear her gaze from those silent records of time's passage, each mark representing a day of lost freedom, of suffering. Some tallies were short, others stretched on and on, disappearing into the shadows in the corner of the ceiling.

"Three months," Vidia answered, her voice flat. "Though my sentence is apparently two years. For defending myself." The bitterness in her tone was subtle but unmistakable.

"I've done seven months in this hole," Soren said flatly, sitting back on her bunk. "Five more to go – allegedly. Though it feels like years. Time moves differently down here, away from the sun and moon."

"They haven't told me how long I've got," Lilyana said.

"Don't hold your breath," Soren said cynically. "They'll take their time telling you anything worth knowing – and even then, they can't be trusted to keep their word. There's no such thing as a solid release date in here."

"Is there any way out?" Lilyana asked, lowering her voice to barely above a whisper. The question felt dangerous, rebellious even in its asking. "I mean, besides serving whatever arbitrary sentence they've given us?"

Soren snorted. "Planning your escape already? I like your spirit. But no, there's no way out. The prison is underground, as you've noticed. The only exit is through the vampire quarters above, and that's firmly secured. Even if you somehow managed to get in, the academy is surrounded by a twenty-foot wall topped with silver spikes, monitored by surveillance and guards. The entire prison is warded against fae magic. Your natural abilities are suppressed here – no light manipulation, no plant communication, no air current control.

Whatever skills your bloodline has, they're useless within these walls."

"Someone must have escaped before," Lilyana persisted, unwilling to accept such absolute hopelessness. "In all the years this place has existed, someone must have found a way."

"There are stories," Vidia admitted, glancing towards the door as if fearing to be overheard. "Whispers among the prisoners about a fae who made it out three years ago. They say she discovered an old drainage tunnel that had been forgotten during renovations. But that's all they are – stories to keep hope alive."

A loud buzzer suddenly blared through the block, the harsh electronic sound penetrating every corner, causing Lilyana to jump and hit her head on the low ceiling. The pain was sharp but brief, just one more discomfort to add to the catalogue her body was already experiencing.

"Evening meal," Vidia explained, standing and stretching as much as the small cell would allow. "The food here is barely edible, but it's sustenance, and you'll need your strength."

The cell door slid open automatically with that same hydraulic hiss, joining a chorus of similar sounds throughout the block as all doors opened simultaneously. Prisoners began filing out towards the centre of the block where tables were arranged in long rows, bolted to the floor to prevent their use as weapons or barricades. Guards watched from elevated platforms, shock batons visible at their sides, their expressions ranging from vigilant to openly hostile.

Dinner was a grey, tasteless gruel served in metal bowls, accompanied by a piece of hard bread that might have been fresh days ago. A cup of tepid water completed the meagre meal. Lilyana struggled to swallow it.

"You'll get used to it," Soren said, noticing her difficulty. "Or you won't. Some don't." She nodded towards a thin fae sitting alone at the end of a table.

As Lilyana forced herself to eat the bland meal, ignoring the occasional gritty texture that suggested the kitchen's cleaning standards were as low as everything else in this place, she observed the dynamics of the prison. There were clear factions among the inmates – some clustering together for protection, their heads bent close in whispered conversation, others isolating themselves, watchful and wary. The guards watched it all with varying degrees of amusement and contempt, occasionally calling out a prisoner for some perceived infraction, their voices carrying easily in the cavernous space.

One guard in particular caught her attention – a female vampire with platinum hair pulled back in a severe bun, her uniform more elaborate than the others, with additional insignia on the collar. She stood on the highest observation platform, her posture perfectly straight, her gaze sweeping systematically across the dining area. Unlike the others, she didn't openly taunt the prisoners or engage in casual cruelty, but there was something calculating in her gaze that Lilyana found even more disturbing – a cold intelligence that seemed to note and categorise every interaction, every potential weakness.

"That's Warden Isolde," Vidia whispered, following Lilyana's gaze. "She's the worst of them all. She believes fae are deeply inferior and need to be controlled. She has theories about fae rehabilitation through systematic discipline. This entire prison is her playground."

Lilyana suppressed a shudder as the warden's gaze passed over their table, lingering momentarily on the new arrival before moving on. In that brief moment of eye contact, Lilyana saw something that chilled her more than any open threat – a curious interest, as if the warden had identified her as a subject worthy of special attention.

After dinner, prisoners were allowed one hour of so-called recreation in the block's central area before being locked down for the night. This seemed to consist mainly of the freedom to move about the open space rather than being confined to cells, with little actual recreational activities available. Some prisoners exercised. Others gathered in small groups, conversing in hushed tones. A few simply sat alone, staring into space with vacant expressions that suggested their minds had retreated to places their bodies could not follow.

Lilyana sat with her cellmates on a bench against a wall, observing and learning. In prison, she was quickly realising, knowledge was as valuable as any physical resource – knowing the unwritten rules, the power dynamics, the dangerous personalities to avoid.

"See that group?" Soren pointed discreetly to a cluster of five fae with various coloured wings, all sitting close together on the floor in a corner. They ranged in age from a young girl who couldn't have been more than eighteen to an elderly fae whose deep purple wings had seen better days. Despite their differences, there was a clear bond between them, evident in the protective way the older members positioned themselves around the younger ones. "They're the Sisterhood. They look out for each other. Not a bad group to align with, if they'll have you. They're selective though."

"And them?" Lilyana nodded towards three muscular fae, their wings held high and proud, the membranes scarred but unbowed.

They stood rather than sat, their faces marked with recent bruises, their expressions defiant despite their obvious discomfort. They looked tough, rebellious – almost unafraid, but not quite.

"The Thorns," Vidia explained, her voice dropping even lower. "Troublemakers. They resist, fight back when they can. They've all spent time in "special discipline" – that's what the guards call the punishment cells on the lowest level. No light down there at all, just darkness and cold. They spend more time in solitary than anyone, but they don't care. Some say they're suicidal, others reckon they're the only ones with any dignity left."

"What about him?" Lilyana had noticed a lone male fae with iridescent green wings – scarred, ragged, and uneven, as if damaged by some past trauma – sitting apart from everyone, his back to the wall, his eyes constantly scanning the space with methodical precision. Unlike most prisoners, who seemed diminished by their captivity, he exuded a contained energy, a watchfulness that spoke of a mind constantly at work. "He doesn't seem to belong to a group."

"Ferrin," Vidia said, lowering her voice to barely above a breath. "He's been here a long time. He tried to escape once and nearly made it to the outer wall before they caught him. The guards made an example of him – kept him in solitary for months, brought him out only for "public discipline sessions". He hasn't spoken a word to anyone since they brought him back to general population."

Soren's expression shifted, showing a rare moment of genuine concern. "Stay away from him, Lilyana. Not because he's dangerous to you, but because the guards watch him constantly. Anyone who associates with him gets extra attention, and trust me, that's the last thing you want in here."

As the recreation hour ended and prisoners were herded back to their cells, Lilyana caught Ferrin looking at her. For a brief moment, their eyes met across the corridor – luminous pink meeting intense emerald – and she saw something in his gaze that made her breath catch. Not the deadness she'd observed in many others, but a carefully banked fire, a purpose hidden beneath layers of caution. He nodded almost imperceptibly, a gesture so subtle it might have been her imagination, before turning away and walking with measured steps towards his cell.

Back in her cell, as the lights dimmed to near darkness for the night cycle, leaving only the faintest glow from emergency lights in the corridor outside, Lilyana lay on her bunk, her mind racing despite her physical exhaustion. She thought of home, of freedom. She thought of her mother, probably wondering what had happened to her daughter. Would anyone tell her?

"Try to sleep," Vidia advised from below, her voice gentle in the darkness. "First night's the hardest. It gets... not better, exactly, but more familiar. Routine is survival in here."

"Why do we let them do this to us?" Lilyana whispered into the darkness, the question burning in her chest. She kept her voice low, aware that sound carried in the quiet cell block. "There are so many more fae than vampires. If we all rose up together, united..."

"Save that kind of talk," Soren cut in sharply from across the small space, her voice carrying a warning edge. "The walls have ears, and that's how you get your wings clipped. And a fae without wings is barely alive, as you well know."

The threat of wing-clipping hung heavily in the silence that followed. For fae, wings weren't just appendages for flight – they were identity, freedom, connection to their heritage and to each other. The complex patterns of colour and texture were as unique as fingerprints, markers of family lineage and personal history. To lose them was to lose everything that made them who they were, to become ghosts of themselves, forever grounded.

"Just focus on surviving," Vidia said softly after a long moment. There was a rustling below as she shifted on her bunk. "One day at a time. That's all any of us can do."

But as Lilyana drifted into an uneasy sleep, her thoughts weren't of survival – at least, not merely survival. They were of escape, of freedom. There had to be a way out of this place, and she was determined to find it. The arbitrary cruelty of imprisonment only strengthened her resolve. If there was no justice in the system, then she owed the system nothing – not compliance, not acceptance, certainly not resignation to her fate.

Chapter Three

Three weeks into her imprisonment, Lilyana had learnt the rhythms of Grindmore Prison Academy with painful intimacy. Every day followed the same punishing schedule, designed not merely for containment but for the systematic crushing of spirit and will. The day began harshly at five AM to the ear-splitting screech of industrial alarms that jolted prisoners from whatever brief reprieve sleep had offered. Guards would storm through the cell block, batons slapping against metal bars to amplify the cacophony, ensuring that even the deepest sleeper was rudely thrust into consciousness.

Standing rigid for morning inspection followed – a full thirty minutes of absolute stillness while guards scrutinised every prisoner for infractions real or imagined. The slightest twitch of a wing or flicker of defiance in a prisoner's eyes could earn them a shock baton to the ribs or worse.

Breakfast consisted of watery porridge that tasted of dishwater and resignation, served in metal bowls that were perpetually stained with the meals of prisoners past.

Four gruelling hours of "re-education" lectures on proper fae subservience came next, held in a chamber whose very architecture seemed designed to diminish – low ceilings that forced taller fae to stoop and seats positioned to make wing-folding as uncomfortable as possible. The lectures themselves were mind-numbing exercises in propaganda, delivered by vampire instructors who spoke of fae as if discussing an inferior species of bacteria rather than sentient beings.

Lunch provided little respite – bland soup with occasional unidentifiable floating bits and stale bread hard enough to chip teeth. This inadequate sustenance was meant to fuel the afternoon's forced labour in the laundry, where steam and chemicals created a suffocating atmosphere. Dinner was hardly worth the name, followed by a single, precious hour of recreation – a mockery of freedom. Then came lockdown by nine PM, when cells darkened and silence was enforced with brutal efficiency.

Life in the prison found countless ways to break a fae's spirit – to hammer home the message that they were lesser, that resistance was futile, that submission was the only path to survival.

Today, Lilyana sat hunched at her assigned station in the laundry, feeding endless sheets into industrial washing machines that roared and vibrated like hungry beasts. The air hung thick with steam that beaded on her skin and plastered strands of hair to her forehead, while the harsh chemical smell of industrial detergent burned her nostrils and left an acrid taste coating her tongue. Each breath felt like drawing in liquid rather than air. Around her, other prisoners moved with the slow, deliberate motions of the perpetually exhausted, their once-vibrant wings now dulled by captivity and poor nutrition.

Guards in crisp uniforms patrolled the aisles between workstations with predatory alertness, their shock batons held at the ready. They seemed to derive particular pleasure from striking prisoners who worked too slowly with crackling electric jolts that left muscles spasming for hours afterwards. Their boots clicked against the concrete floor, a metronomic reminder of authority and the ever-present threat of violence.

"Psst... Lilyana."

Lilyana glanced sideways, careful to keep the movement subtle enough to avoid drawing attention. At the next station stood Soren, her blue wings folded tightly against her back – a defensive posture to avoid giving the supervisor any excuse for "corrective measures".

"What?" Lilyana whispered in response, her fingers never ceasing their mechanical task of feeding sheets into the voracious machine. Steam billowed around her hands, scalding her skin and raising angry red blotches that would join the collection of similar marks she'd accumulated over the weeks.

"Meeting tonight. Recreation hour. The Sisterhood wants to talk to you." Soren's voice barely carried over the thunderous rumble of the machinery, yet she still darted nervous glances towards the nearest guard, a burly vampire known for his enthusiasm with the shock baton.

Lilyana raised an eyebrow but didn't immediately respond, weighing the implications of this invitation. In the political landscape of Grindmore, alliances were as necessary as they were dangerous. She'd been meticulously careful these past few weeks, observing the various factions that had formed among the prisoners without overtly aligning herself with any. The Sisterhood, a tightly-knit group of female fae prisoners, had been watching her too, she knew. Unlike some of the more opportunistic groups that accepted any prisoner desperate for protection, they were notably selective about who they associated with, operating with a discretion and discipline that had earned them a grudging respect even from some of the guards. Lilyana had noted their movements, their methods, the way they communicated through looks and gestures, and she was intensely curious as to why they'd taken an interest in her specifically.

"Eyes on your work!" A guard barked from behind them, his voice carrying the distinctive aristocratic inflection of the upper vampire classes. He punctuated his command by slapping his baton against a metal table with a threatening crack that echoed like a gunshot through the humid room. Several prisoners flinched involuntarily, their wings giving telltale twitches of alarm. "The next one who speaks gets a personal lesson in discipline. Perhaps in the private instruction room."

The mention of the "private instruction room" – a euphemism for the soundproofed chamber where particularly brutal punishments were administered – sent a ripple of tension through the nearby prisoners. Lilyana ducked her head and continued working with renewed intensity, her fingers moving faster through the pile of damp sheets, but her mind was racing behind her carefully crafted mask of compliance.

Since her arrival at Grindmore, she'd been systematically mapping the prison in her head, creating a mental blueprint of corridors, chambers, and restricted areas. She'd noted guard rotations with obsessive attention to detail, tracking which guards appeared during which shifts, who was prone to distraction, who was particularly vigilant. She'd observed which doors required physical keys and which used electronic locks with keycards or numeric codes, memorising digits when possible by watching guards' fingers on keypads. She'd learnt which guards were merely cruel and which were genuinely observant, which were susceptible to flattery or bribery, which were impervious to any form of manipulation.

The key to escape, she'd realised during her second week, wasn't just about finding a physical way out – it was about constructing a complex web of knowledge: knowing who to trust, who to avoid, who to fear, and who might be manipulated into helping, whether knowingly or not. It was about understanding the social dynamics of Grindmore as intimately as its architectural layout. In a place designed to strip away individuality and reduce prisoners to numbers, information had become her most precious currency.

That evening during recreation hour, Lilyana approached the far corner of the common area where the Sisterhood usually gathered, their unofficial territory respected by the other prisoners. This recreation space was a grim parody of leisure – a rectangular room with cracked linoleum flooring, flickering fluorescent lights that buzzed incessantly, and a few battered tables and benches bolted to the floor. The walls were an institutional grey that had faded to a sickly yellow in places, adorned only by motivational posters extolling the virtues of compliance and the occasional stain that the cleaning crews had given up trying to remove.

Five fae women of various ages sat on the benches in a loose circle, positioning themselves to maintain clear sightlines of the entire room – a defensive formation that spoke of years of practiced vigilance. Their wings – ranging from Thalia's deep purple to Ember's fiery orange-red gradients, with shades of teal, amber, and violet in between – created a vibrant display that stood in stark contrast to the drab prison surroundings. Each pair of wings told its own story of hardship; some bore the distinctive notches of guard "discipline", others displayed the uneven growth that resulted from long-term nutritional deficiencies.

"Lilyana," Thalia greeted. The eldest woman in the group, her deep purple wings bore extensive evidence of past damage that had healed poorly, leaving asymmetrical patterns and limiting her mobility. Her face, once beautiful, was now mapped with the fine lines of age and stress, but her eyes remained sharp and evaluating. "Join us."

Lilyana sat cautiously on the edge of the bench, acutely aware that other inmates across the recreation area were watching this interaction with thinly veiled interest. New alliances in Grindmore were rare enough to warrant attention, especially when they involved the exclusive Sisterhood. She felt the weight of dozens of pairs of eyes on her back, noticed the subtle drop in conversation volume as prisoners strained to overhear.

"We've been observing you," Thalia continued without preamble, her voice carrying the slight rasp of someone who had screamed herself hoarse too many times in the past. "You're different from most new arrivals. You watch. You listen. You plan.

While others waste energy raging against their captivity or collapse into despair, you've maintained a calculating stillness."

"I'm just trying to survive," Lilyana replied carefully, her tone neutral despite the rapid beating of her heart. The Sisterhood's interest could be a lifeline or a trap, and she couldn't yet determine which.

Ember, the younger fae with flame-coloured wings, laughed softly, the sound containing little mirth. Her wing tips flickered with tiny sparks – a rare phenomenon among fire-aspected fae that the wards of the prison should have suppressed. "We all start that way, Lilyana. Every single one of us arrived thinking just about survival. But you're thinking beyond survival, aren't you? You're thinking about freedom."

Lilyana tensed involuntarily, the muscles along her spine and wing joints tightening. Freedom was more than just a dangerous thought in Grindmore – it was practically a forbidden word, one that guards punished merely for uttering aloud. To have someone speak it so directly, even in the relative privacy of recreation hour, felt simultaneously liberating and terrifying.

"Freedom is a dangerous thought in here," Lilyana responded, keeping her expression neutral though her pink eyes darted briefly to the nearest guard, ensuring he wasn't within earshot.

"That's precisely why we're interested in you," Thalia said, leaning forward slightly, her voice dropping to a near-whisper. "Dangerous thoughts are exactly what we cultivate. The vampires can bind our wings, work our bodies to exhaustion, even punish our smallest infractions, but they cannot chain our minds unless we allow it."

Before Lilyana could respond, a shadow fell across their circle, accompanied by a sudden drop in temperature that raised goosebumps along her arms. Looking up, she found herself staring into the cold, assessing eyes of Warden Isolde. Up close, the vampire's sinister beauty was even more striking and unsettling – porcelain skin without a single visible pore, platinum hair arranged in an immaculate chignon without a strand out of place, and eyes the colour of arctic ice that seemed to see through flesh to the vulnerabilities beneath.

"What a touching gathering," the vampire said, her voice like silk over steel, each syllable precisely enunciated with the cultured accent of aristocratic vampires. "The Sisterhood welcomes a new member? How charming."

"Just passing the time, Warden," Thalia replied, her tone carefully respectful despite the defiance that smouldered in her eyes. Her wings folded tighter against her back, a subconscious attempt to make herself a smaller target.

Warden Isolde's penetrating gaze shifted to Lilyana, studying her with an unnerving intensity that felt like invisible fingers probing beneath her skin, searching for weakness. "How are you finding your re-education, two-four-seven?" She deliberately used Lilyana's prison number rather than her name – one of the many dehumanising tactics employed by the guards, a constant reminder that in this place, individuality was not a right.

"Enlightening, Warden," Lilyana answered, matching Thalia's careful balance of respect and resistance. She kept her posture deliberately relaxed despite the instinctive urge to shrink away from the vampire's proximity. To show fear was to invite intimidation.

"Is it, now?" With calculated intimacy, Warden Isolde reached out and deliberately brushed her fingertips against the sensitive junction where Lilyana's wings met her back, causing an involuntary shudder of revulsion. "Because I've noticed you spend more time watching than learning. Curious eyes can be dangerous – to their owner."

The threat hung in the air, unmistakable in its oblique delivery. Lilyana kept her gaze fixed forward, refusing to show fear despite the cold dread pooling in her stomach. She was acutely aware of how vulnerable her wings were with the warden standing behind her – a quick, vicious twist could cause damage that would never properly heal, as evidenced by many of the long-term prisoners.

"I'm simply trying to understand the rules, Warden. To avoid further... misunderstandings." She chose her words with extreme care, each one balanced on a knife-edge between submission and dignity.

Warden Isolde laughed coldly, the sound entirely devoid of humour, more akin to glass breaking than to genuine exuberance. "The only rule you need to understand is that you are nothing. Less than nothing. Your freedom, your dignity, even those pretty pink wings of yours – all exist at our pleasure." She leaned close to Lilyana's ear, close enough that her unnaturally cold breath raised chills along her neck. "Remember that, two-four-seven. Everything you believe belongs to you – your thoughts, your hope, your very identity – can be taken. Some prisoners need several demonstrations before this lesson takes root."

As the warden straightened and walked away with predatory grace, her heels clicking a measured cadence against the floor, Lilyana remembered to breathe. The encounter had lasted less than a minute but had left her feeling as drained as a full shift in the laundry.

"She's taken an interest in you," Thalia observed grimly once the warden was out of earshot. "That's rarely good. The last prisoner who caught her attention spent two weeks in solitary confinement. When he returned, his wings were..." She didn't finish the sentence, but her expression conveyed enough.

"She knows," Ember added, her voice hushed but intense. "She senses you're not broken yet. That makes you either a challenge or a threat in her eyes. Neither position is enviable."

"Which brings us back to why we wanted to speak with you," continued another member of the Sisterhood, a quiet woman named Nella with teal wings that shimmered with subtle iridescence even under the harsh prison lighting. Her delicate features belied an inner strength evident in her steady gaze. "We have... resources. Information. Things that might interest someone with observant eyes such as yours."

Lilyana glanced around the recreation area, performing a careful sweep to take in the positions of all the guards and ensuring no unwelcome prisoners were within earshot. Only when satisfied did she lean slightly closer. "What kind of information?"

"Guard rotations. Blind spots in surveillance. Which doors are checked frequently and which might remain unnoticed if tampered with. Which guards can be bribed or distracted and with what currency." Thalia's voice was barely above a whisper, the words formed more by lip movements than actual sound. "We've been here a long time, collecting these pieces, fitting together the puzzle of Grindmore's weaknesses."

"Why share them with me?" Lilyana asked suspiciously, searching their faces for signs of deception. In her three weeks at Grindmore, she'd already witnessed multiple betrayals among prisoners – some for favours as minor as shower privileges.

"Because we recognise the look in your eyes," Ember said, her gaze direct and unflinching. "It's the same look Ferrin had before..." She trailed off, glancing meaningfully towards the green-winged male fae sitting alone at the far end of the recreation area, his wings bearing the distinctive scarring of severe punishment.

She didn't need to finish her sentence. Lilyana understood the reference immediately. Before his escape attempt. Before he had nearly made it beyond the prison's outer wall only to be recaptured and subjected to what must have been excruciating treatment.

"You want to help me escape?" she asked, keeping her incredulity contained to a whisper. "Why? Why not use this information yourselves? If you've been gathering it for so long..."

Thalia's expression grew solemn, the lines on her face deepening as she flexed her injured wings slightly, drawing attention to their limited mobility. "Some of us are too old, too damaged for the physical demands of escape. These wings will never again sustain flight strong enough to clear the outer walls." Her voice carried the pain of bitter acceptance, of dreams long surrendered to reality.

"Others have family inside they won't leave behind," added a Sisterhood member Lilyana hadn't met before, a woman with amber wings and hollow cheeks who glanced meaningfully towards a younger fae across the room. The family resemblance was unmistakable – they shared the same distinctive wing pattern and facial structure, likely mother and daughter.

"But everyone needs hope, Lilyana," Thalia continued, her weathered hand briefly touching Lilyana's in a gesture so quick it would appear accidental to any watching guard. "The story of someone who made it out... that would be worth everything. Even to those who remain behind."

"And you think I could be that someone?" Lilyana couldn't keep the scepticism from her voice. She was a newcomer, untested, lacking the institutional knowledge that came with years of imprisonment.

"We think you have the best chance we've seen in years," Nella said, her teal wings giving a subtle flutter that conveyed emphasis in fae body language. "You're observant, patient, and most importantly, you haven't given up. The prison hasn't got inside your head yet, hasn't convinced you that this is all there is, all there can ever be."

Lilyana considered their words carefully, analysing them from every angle. Trust was a rare and precious commodity in Grindmore, as scarce as sunlight in these underground corridors. Betrayal was always possible, perhaps even probable. The Sisterhood's offer could be genuine, or it could be an elaborate trap, a test of her loyalty orchestrated by the warden herself.

Yet something in their expressions, in the desperate hope barely concealed beneath their carefully maintained composure, rang true. These were women who had endured more than Lilyana could imagine and still maintained some fragment of resistance in their hearts. That alone deserved respect.

"I'll need more than information," she said finally, her decision made. "I'll need..."

"Rec time's over!" A guard's voice boomed across the block. "Back to your cells, maggots! Any prisoner not moving in five seconds gets a personal escort!"

As prisoners began shuffling towards their cells with the resigned movements of the institutionalised, Thalia quickly pressed something into Lilyana's palm with a practiced sleight of hand. "Tomorrow. Laundry shift. Check the steam pipe behind sorting station three."

Lilyana closed her fingers around the object – a small piece of folded paper – and slipped it into her sleeve with a subtle movement before any guards could notice. Her heart pounded with a mixture of fear and exhilaration as she moved towards the exit, careful to maintain the properly submissive posture expected during movement between prison areas.

Later, locked in her cell with Soren and Vidia, Lilyana waited for the lights to dim and the guard patrol to pass before carefully unfolding the paper under her blanket. She used the soft pink glow from her eyes to examine what turned out to be a crude but detailed map of a section of the prison she hadn't seen before: a maintenance tunnel that appeared to connect the laundry facility to a storage area near the kitchen.

The map included notations that took her several minutes to decipher – symbols indicating guard patrol frequencies, and what appeared to be time windows when the area might be least monitored. The level of detail suggested years of patient observation and information gathering, confirming that the Sisterhood's intelligence network within Grindmore was far more sophisticated than most probably realised.

"Making friends with the Sisterhood?" Soren asked from her bunk, failing to maintain a casual tone, unable to conceal her interest.

Lilyana refolded the paper and tucked it into a small tear she'd made in her mattress, a hiding place she'd been saving for something of value. "Just getting to know people. Seems important in a place like this."

"Be careful," Vidia warned. "The Sisterhood have years of experience between them. They've survived because they understand the true currency of Grindmore: information. They've seen many come and go, attempting what you're thinking about."

Lilyana looked down sharply, surprised by the directness of the comment. "I never said..."

"You didn't have to," Vidia replied. "It's in everything you do – the way you watch the guards, how you observe steps between doors. We've seen it before. That first phase of imprisonment, when escape seems possible, when the mind hasn't accepted the permanence of captivity."

Soren approached silently on bare feet and hoisted herself onto the edge of Lilyana's bunk, the thin mattress barely dipping beneath her weight. "Don't make assumptions about who's a friend and who's a foe in here. Survival makes monsters out of all of us."

Lilyana studied her cellmate's face in the dim light. "Are you saying I shouldn't trust you?"

"I'm saying trust is a luxury none of us can afford," Soren replied, the bitter pragmatism in her voice hinting at lessons learnt through painful experience. "Some vampires like to pit us against each other. Betraying another fae is sometimes the only way to avoid punishment. The system is designed to ensure that no prisoner can fully trust another."

"Have you betrayed others?" Lilyana asked directly, needing to understand the woman with whom she shared such close quarters.

Soren's blue wings fluttered slightly in the darkness – a subtle but unmistakable sign of discomfort. "I've had to survive in this hell. Draw your own conclusions."

With that, she returned to her own bunk, leaving Lilyana to ponder her words in the darkness. The statement was neither a confirmation nor a denial, but it spoke volumes about the reality of Grindmore and the choices it forced upon its inhabitants.

Sleep came fitfully that night. Lilyana's dreams were haunted by endless corridors that shifted and changed each time she thought she'd found a way out, by the guards' sadistic laughter echoing from every direction at once, by the sensation of her wings being slowly, methodically broken joint by joint.

Chapter Four

The next day during laundry duty, Lilyana manoeuvred with deliberate casualness to be assigned to the sorting station near the steam pipe Thalia had mentioned. She worked diligently for over an hour, establishing a rhythm of productivity that satisfied the watching guards, before implementing her plan. Timing her movements to coincide with a guard shift change – a three-minute window when attention was typically divided – she deliberately dropped a stack of sheets, creating a minor disruption.

As she bent to retrieve them, seemingly flustered and apologetic, she quickly checked behind the steam pipe and found a small package wrapped in laundry rags, concealed in the narrow gap between the pipe and the wall. She palmed the package and incorporated it into the bundle of fallen sheets.

Back at her workstation, she carefully unwrapped the package under the pretence of folding sheets. Inside was a contraband item so valuable she nearly gasped aloud – a small vial of venom. Not enough to kill, but enough to temporarily paralyse a vampire. It represented both tremendous risk and opportunity. Possession of anything that could impair vampire physiology carried the severest penalties.

Throughout the following days, more information and small contraband items appeared in hiding spots around the prison – a hand-drawn map of the ventilation system with measurements noted for each shaft and junction, a small lock-picking tool fashioned from a laundry machine part worn thin and shaped through months of patient work.

The Sisterhood was methodically providing her with the tools for escape, but Lilyana remained cautious, testing each piece of information before trusting it completely. She verified guard rotations herself, counting seconds between patrols and comparing them with the Sisterhood's information. She examined lock mechanisms surreptitiously, confirming they matched the descriptions provided. Each piece of intelligence that proved accurate built her confidence incrementally, though she maintained her scepticism as a defensive measure.

One evening, as she returned from the showers, she found Ferrin waiting near her cell, apparently engaged in conversation with Soren. Both fell silent as she approached, an abrupt cessation that raised immediate suspicion in Lilyana's mind. Ferrin's posture was tense, his green wings held unnaturally still in a way that bespoke either extreme control or extreme anxiety.

"Lilyana," he greeted her. "I've heard you're interested in architecture."

She understood the coded language immediately. Architecture – the structure of the prison, escape routes, the building's vulnerabilities. "I've developed an appreciation for it recently," she replied carefully, studying his face for any sign of duplicity. His eyes were clear but guarded, giving away nothing of his true intentions.

"I worked in construction before my imprisonment," he said, his green wings shifting slightly, revealing glimpses of the extensive scarring that marked their undersides – more evidence of the brutal punishment that had followed his failed escape attempt. "Perhaps we could discuss it sometime. I've particular knowledge of load-bearing structures and... exit designs."

"I'd like that," Lilyana responded, maintaining an outward casualness that belied the racing of her heart. Ferrin represented both tremendous risk and potential reward – he had attempted escape and failed, which meant he knew routes and mistakes to avoid, but his failure also marked him as potentially compromised, possibly even working with the guards to identify other escape attempts.

After Ferrin left, Lilyana turned to Soren with a questioning look, searching her cellmate's face for any hint of what had transpired before her arrival.

"Don't," Soren warned immediately, her voice a harsh whisper as she retreated to the far corner of their cell. "Don't ask what that was about, and don't trust him. Not with anything you can't afford to have the guards know."

"Why? Because he tried to escape?" Lilyana countered, keeping her own voice low as she sat on her bunk, angling her body to block her mouth from potential observation. "That should mean he has valuable information."

"Because he failed," Soren urged, her eyes intense with warning. "And because despite the punishment, he hasn't broken yet. Either he's insane, or..."

"Or he's working for the vampires now," Vidia finished quietly from her bunk, where she lay curled beneath a thin blanket. "They do that, you know. Take someone who's attempted escape and force them to become informants. Who better to identify escape plots than someone who's tried it themselves?"

The possibility hadn't occurred to Lilyana with such explicit clarity before, but now it seemed blindingly obvious. A prisoner who had attempted escape would be the perfect informant for the guards – someone who could identify others with similar intentions, who would recognise the telltale signs of planning, the collection of materials, the subtle changes in behaviour that preceded an attempt.

Yet something about Ferrin seemed genuine. The fire she'd glimpsed in his eyes. There had been a defiant spark there, carefully hidden but still burning beneath layers of caution and pain. Or perhaps that was merely what she wanted to see – a reflection of her own determination rather than the reality of a broken man playing a role assigned by his captors.

"I'll be careful," she promised her cellmates, the words both an acknowledgment of their warning and a subtle assertion that she would make her own judgment about Ferrin's trustworthiness.

That night, unable to sleep, Lilyana stared at the ceiling of their cell, her mind working through the pieces of the puzzle she'd been gathering with methodical precision. The prison's layout, the guard rotations, the security measures, the weak points in surveillance – she was beginning to see a pattern, a potential pathway through Grindmore's labyrinthine defences.

But she still lacked one crucial element – a key to the locked door that separated the prison's underground levels from the vampire quarters above. Unlike many other security points in the facility, which had transitioned to electronic systems with keycards or numeric pads, that particular door required an actual physical key. From what she'd gathered through careful questioning and observation, Warden Isolde was responsible for that particular key – a final obstacle between imprisonment and potential freedom.

Lilyana's mind refused to settle. Without the key, escape was impossible; relying on a lock pick in that part of the prison would be far too dangerous. And yet, she couldn't shake the feeling that a solution was just out of reach, waiting to be uncovered. Her thoughts swirled until exhaustion finally won out, and as sleep claimed her, she dreamed – not of cold stone walls and locked doors, but of open skies and freedom.

Chapter Five

Weeks had passed since Lilyana's covert meetings with the Sisterhood. The small vial of venom remained unopened, returned to its hiding place behind the steam pipe, nestled in a crevice where the ancient metal met crumbling mortar. The lock-picking tool, meticulously drawn maps, and other carefully collected contraband had all been returned to their original locations – hidden in plain sight among everyday objects or secreted away in the countless forgotten corners of the prison. To anyone watching – and many were, with calculating eyes that missed little – Lilyana appeared to have surrendered completely to her fate, another broken spirit accepting the inevitability of captivity.

It hadn't been an easy decision. Every morning as she stood for inspection, wings folded submissively behind her back, shoulders bent in practiced deference, a part of her raged against the pretence. The fiery core of her being burned with indignation, demanding action, resistance, anything but this charade of submission. But another part – the calculating, patient part honed by observation and planning – knew this performance of defeat was her only real chance at freedom.

The Sisterhood had been too visible, their assistance too conspicuous. Lilyana had noticed Warden Isolde's penetrating gaze following her with increasing frequency after her interactions with Thalia and the others, those cold eyes narrowing with suspicion at every whispered conversation. Ferrin's attention had also been too dangerous – whether he was truly a fellow prisoner planning another escape attempt or an informant bullied by the guards into identifying potential troublemakers, his interest had also marked her as someone to watch, someone who warranted extra scrutiny.

So Lilyana had withdrawn into a carefully constructed shell of compliance. She spoke less during meals, her once-animated conversations reduced to monosyllabic responses. She kept her head down during labour shifts, completing her assigned tasks with mechanical efficiency. She even participated with apparent sincerity during the daily "re-education" lectures, dutifully paying attention to the supposed inherent inferiority of faekind. She'd stopped mapping guard rotations in plain sight, ceased visibly counting steps between security checkpoints, and abandoned her habit of overtly watching for which doors required keycards versus physical keys.

Or at least, she appeared to have stopped, while her mental catalogue of the prison's workings grew more detailed by the day.

"You're doing the right thing," Vidia said one night as they lay in their bunks.

"What do you mean?" Lilyana asked, feigning ignorance though she knew exactly what Vidia was referring to.

"Giving up on... you know..." Vidia whispered. "Escape fantasies never end well. Everyone who tries ends up worse off than before."

Soren's bitter laugh cut through the darkness, harsh and hollow, suggesting she had lost hope long ago. "You think wing-binders hurt? Those metal clips digging into your flight muscles? Imagine how bad wing-clipping would be. Permanent. Irreversible."

Lilyana suppressed a shudder that threatened to reveal too much of her true feelings. "I've come to my senses," she said, the lie practiced enough now to sound sincere, even to her own ears. "Maybe someday I'll be released. Maybe we all will."

"That's the spirit," Soren said with resigned sarcasm, shifting on her bunk. "Just keep your head down, do what they say, and maybe in ten or twenty years, they'll let you out to live the remaining decades of your life as a broken, compliant little butterfly."

"Soren," Vidia chided gently, her voice carrying a maternal softness that seemed out of place in the harsh prison environment.

"No, she's right," Lilyana said, staring up at the ceiling where the tally marks of previous occupants stood as mute testimony to time wasted behind these walls, each scratch a day someone would never get back. "It's resignation or insanity in here. I choose resignation. At least that way, I get to keep what's left of my mind."

As her cellmates drifted off to sleep, their breathing eventually settling into the rhythm of unconsciousness, Lilyana remained awake, her mind alert despite her body's exhaustion. Their conversation had only strengthened her resolve. The resignation in their voices – the despair disguised as acceptance – was precisely what she wanted to fight against. Needed to fight against. Not just for herself, but for her family and friends on the outside, who must be missing her by now; for the life of freedom that had once been hers, however limited it had been under the brutal reign of the vampires.

The revelation both saddened and inspired her: her cellmates' hopelessness meant they were no longer watching her with suspicion; they had accepted her conversion to compliance. The guards, too, had relaxed their vigilance, no longer shadowing her movements with the same intensity. Even Warden Isolde's cruel attention had shifted to other, more defiant prisoners whose resistance was more obvious, more direct, and ultimately more futile.

In the quiet darkness, a smile curved Lilyana's lips, invisible to anyone who might be watching through the door's small observation window. For the first time since her imprisonment, she had achieved something invaluable: invisibility. And invisible prisoners could observe, plan, and ultimately attempt escape.

Chapter Six

Over the following days, Lilyana's outward compliance continued while her mind worked tirelessly on the single most critical obstacle to her freedom: obtaining Warden Isolde's key. The key would unlock the door between the underground prison and the vampire quarters above – the first step towards the outside world.

Warden Isolde, in her arrogance, had begun to taunt Lilyana, mistaking her compliance for a broken spirit. One morning during inspection, as prisoners stood at attention beside their bunks – wings properly folded, eyes downcast in mandatory deference – the warden paused before Lilyana. A cruel smile played on her bloodless lips, revealing the tip of a fang.

"Two-four-seven," she purred, using Lilyana's prisoner number rather than her name – a constant reminder that to the prison administration, she was a number, not an individual. "You've become quite the model prisoner. You do surprise me."

Lilyana kept her gaze appropriately lowered, focused on the polished tips of Warden Isolde's boots. "Thank you, Warden."

"I had such hopes for you," Warden Isolde continued, eyeing Lilyana like a predator weighing whether its prey was worth the effort of a kill. "Such fire in those pretty pink eyes when you arrived. The defiance in your bearing. The way you asked too many questions. And now look at you – docile as a pet moth drawn to a flame."

Warden Isolde toyed with something around her neck – a golden key suspended on a golden chain. The gesture was deliberate, meant to provoke. Lilyana allowed her eyes to flicker briefly to the key, then back to the floor – just enough to show that the taunt had landed, but not enough to reveal the calculation behind her gaze.

Warden Isolde laughed coldly, the sound echoing off the cell's bare walls. "Yes, this little key. The one thing standing between you and freedom. So close, yet impossibly far." She leaned in, her voice dropping to a whisper that carried the scent of iron – whether from the blood she consumed or from the prison itself, Lilyana couldn't tell. "I wear it always, little fae. Even when I sleep. It never leaves my person. Not for bathing, not for rest, not ever."

Lilyana said nothing, but her mind catalogued the information eagerly, fitting it into the puzzle she was constructing piece by piece. The warden never removed the key – a challenge, but also a constant opportunity. Now she knew exactly where her target would be at all times. The question was no longer one of where to find the key depending on what the warden was doing at any given moment, but how to separate it from its wearer.

"Nothing to say?" Warden Isolde straightened, her pale features forming an expression of disappointment at Lilyana's lack of reaction. "Pity. I almost miss your impertinence. Run along to re-education, two-four-seven. Perhaps today's lesson on "The Natural Inferiority of Faekind" will inspire you. Though I doubt you need much convincing these days."

Lilyana kept her wings folded tightly against her back, her posture submissive and her head bowed – but inside, a fire burned brighter than ever, fuelled rather than extinguished by Warden Isolde's mockery.

Chapter Seven

Three days later, a disruption to the prison routine came unexpectedly. Most of the guard force was called away for a massive arrest operation in the city. The resulting shortage of personnel meant essential prison functions continued with skeleton crews, while non-essential areas were temporarily closed, creating an irregular pattern in the usually clockwork operations of Grindmore.

Lilyana found herself assigned to laundry duty as usual, but under the direct supervision of Warden Isolde rather than the regular guards who normally patrolled the area. Warden Isolde clearly resented the assignment, pacing the perimeter of the humid laundry facility with thinly veiled disgust, occasionally wrinkling her nose at the combination of harsh detergent and body odour that permeated the air.

"Keep those machines running at full capacity," she ordered sharply, her voice carrying over the rumble and hiss of the industrial equipment. "I want this shift's quota completed before personnel return."

The prisoners worked in silent compliance, their movements efficient from the familiarity of repetition. The industrial washers churned clouds of steam and detergent-laden air throughout the room, creating a foggy atmosphere that made visibility poor and breathing laborious. Lilyana maintained her position at her sorting station, mechanically folding clean sheets while her mind raced with observations, noting every detail of this unusual circumstance.

Warden Isolde seemed unusually uncomfortable, repeatedly rubbing her nose and eyes as she patrolled the room's perimeter. At first, Lilyana assumed it was simple annoyance at being assigned to supervise such a menial task, beneath the dignity of her position. But as the shift wore on, the warden's discomfort became more pronounced, impossible to miss even to someone not watching as carefully as Lilyana.

The vampire's normally pale skin had developed an unusual flush across the cheekbones, and she occasionally stifled what sounded like a sneeze, turning away from the prisoners as if to hide this perceived weakness.

When Warden Isolde moved to inspect a washing machine at a station nearby, pausing to check the settings, a realisation struck Lilyana with sudden clarity. The warden wasn't merely uncomfortable or annoyed – she was having an allergic reaction. To what, Lilyana wasn't certain, but something in the laundry facility was clearly affecting her – something the fae prisoners were immune to, but that troubled the vampire's heightened senses.

Lilyana carefully observed which areas seemed to trigger the worst reactions, tracking the pattern of Warden Isolde's movements against the intensity of her symptoms. The drying stations, where heated air circulated through freshly washed fabrics, appeared to cause the most pronounced symptoms. Each time Warden Isolde passed near them, her eyes reddened noticeably and her breathing subtly changed, becoming more shallow and controlled, as if to minimise inhalation.

Spores, Lilyana realised suddenly, the knowledge surfacing from her childhood education. The damp heat of the laundry facility was perfect for growing mould, and despite the harsh chemicals used in washing, some always survived in the steam pipes and machine seals, thriving in the humid environment. To fae, these spores were harmless – many fae homes deliberately cultivated certain beneficial moulds for their medicinal properties and natural dyes. But vampires, with their heightened senses and fundamentally different biology, could have severe reactions – particularly to certain varieties that thrived in warm, damp conditions like those in the prison laundry.

Lilyana filed this information away carefully, adding it to her mental inventory of potential advantages. An allergy was a weakness; if Warden Isolde could be incapacitated by it, even briefly... possibilities unfolded in Lilyana's mind, branching into scenarios she would need to examine later, in the privacy of her thoughts.

Towards the end of the shift, Warden Isolde was visibly relieved to leave the laundry facility, ordering the prisoners back to their cells earlier than scheduled. Her usual meticulous inventory counting was abandoned in favour of a hasty retreat from the irritant-filled air. As they filed out in their ordered line, Lilyana noticed something small and metallic on one of the sorting tables – a contraband hair clip. It had probably fallen out of one of the bedsheets.

With a quick glance to ensure no one was watching, she slid it into her sleeve, feeling its wiry texture against her skin like a promise. A small thing, easily missed – but it could become something far more useful than its original purpose suggested. Just as she herself had become something more driven than the compliant prisoner she appeared to be.

Chapter Eight

Two days passed in a blur of final preparations and mounting anxiety, settling in Lilyana's chest like a cold, heavy stone. Sleep eluded her, replaced by restless planning and the mental rehearsal of every step to come. She had meticulously fashioned the metal hair clip into a crude but functional lock pick. She kept it concealed beneath her sleeve at all times, the cool metal pressing against her skin – a constant reminder of her desperate gambit.

Her plan was deceptively simple in concept, yet frighteningly complex in execution. In her mind's eye, she'd spent hours mapping routes where no electronic locking systems would be encountered, calculating timing, visualising every corridor and junction. She would use her improvised lock pick to navigate through the labyrinthine passages that would lead her towards the space separating the underground fae prison from the vampire quarters situated above at ground level.

To reach ground level, she needed to access an old ventilation shaft hidden behind the kitchen storage area. According to the mental map she'd constructed from her research, the shaft should lead directly to the space separating the prison from the vampire quarters. If her timing was right – and it had to be – she would emerge just as Warden Isolde approached the quarters for her customary few hours of rest between the vampire shifts that kept the prison's rigid schedule functioning.

The most crucial element of her plan rested on a desperate gamble that made her stomach twist with uncertainty: that her fae magic – suppressed by the underground prison's wards – would return once she reached ground level. If it did, she could create a distraction potent enough to momentarily overwhelm Warden Isolde. She would need those precious seconds to steal the key that hung perpetually around the vampire's neck, a taunting promise of freedom.

The moments leading up to Lilyana's escape attempt crawled by with excruciating slowness, each minute stretching into what felt like hours. She stood at rigid attention during the morning inspection, her expression carefully blank as guards scrutinised the prisoners with cold, evaluating eyes. The fluorescent lights buzzed overhead with maddening constancy as she mechanically consumed her bland breakfast. The re-education lectures droned on, the propaganda washing over her without penetrating. Lilyana went through these motions with the same compliant demeanour she'd cultivated for weeks, all whilst remaining hyperaware of each passing second ticking away.

When laundry duty finally arrived in the afternoon rotation, her heart was pounding so loudly she feared the guards might hear it. The laundry facility felt unusually crowded that day, the humid air thick with the smell of industrial detergent and the mechanical rhythm of washing machines. Lilyana worked methodically, sorting fabrics and loading machines, her movements precise while her mind remained laser-focused on the time. The minutes trickled by with agonising lethargy. When the guard at the front finally called for the standard head count, and all eyes and bodies turned forward in practiced unison, Lilyana made her move. With a grace born of urgency, she slipped silently through the door at the back of the laundry, her movements fluid and soundless.

She had done it. The first part of her plan had succeeded, though it felt anything but simple as adrenaline coursed through her veins like liquid fire. Now it was time for the truly dangerous portion: the point of no return. Moving swiftly but cautiously, her footsteps barely audible on the concrete floor, Lilyana navigated the dimly lit kitchen service corridor. She passed the shuttered food dispensary, its metal grates locked tight, and continued towards the storage areas beyond.

The maintenance access point was a small, inconspicuous metal door set into the wall behind tall metal shelves stacked with bags of flour, rice, and other dried goods. The shelves provided perfect cover as she retrieved her lock pick from its hiding place. She knelt before the door, her fingers trembling slightly with a mixture of fear and anticipation as she inserted the bent metal into the keyhole. The lock was relatively simple – designed for keeping out curious prisoners rather than determined escapees. After a tense minute of delicate manipulation, the metal scraping softly against the internal mechanism, she felt the satisfying click of the tumblers releasing their hold.

The door swung open with a soft creak that seemed thunderous in the silence, revealing a narrow, dusty tunnel beyond. Ducking inside quickly, Lilyana pulled the door closed behind her, plunging herself into near-total darkness. Only the ethereal pink glow of her eyes provided any illumination, reflecting dimly off the grimy metal walls of the tunnel and casting eerie shadows that seemed to move of their own accord.

Forcing herself to breathe steadily despite the stale, musty air that filled her lungs, she began to crawl forward on hands and knees. The tunnel was uncomfortably cramped – designed for access to pipes and wiring, not for the passage of bodies, let alone those with wings. The cold, unyielding metal scraped against her palms and legs, and occasionally sharp edges or exposed screws caught at her clothing or the delicate membrane of her wings, causing her to bite back gasps of pain.

She had committed the route to memory through countless nights of visualisation: twenty feet forward through the tunnel, then a left turn at the junction where the pipes branched, followed by another thirty feet of increasingly narrow passage to reach the vertical shaft that would lead upward to the entry point of the vampire quarters.

The junction appeared just where she expected, marked by a rusted sign with faded lettering. She turned left, moving as quickly and quietly as the confined space allowed. She forced her wings to fold as tightly as possible against her back, but they still scraped painfully against the ceiling with every movement. She did her best to ignore it, focusing only on progress and the mental countdown ticking in her head.

When she reached the vertical shaft after navigating around a particularly tight bend, her heart sank momentarily at what she saw. It was narrower than she had anticipated from her information gathering – barely wide enough for her shoulders, let alone her wings that, even tightly folded, still extended several inches from her back. To ascend, she would need to fold her wings painfully tight against her spine and use the maintenance ladder bolted to one side, its metal rungs coated in years of grime and neglect.

There was no time for hesitation or second thoughts. Steeling herself, Lilyana folded her wings until they burned with the unnatural position, the delicate joints protesting the confinement. She grasped the first rung of the ladder, testing its strength before committing her full weight to the climb. Satisfied it would hold, she began to ascend, one cautious rung at a time.

Each step of the ladder brought her closer to ground level – closer to either freedom or disaster with no middle ground between the two possible outcomes. The shaft seemed endless in the oppressive darkness, the only sounds her increasingly laboured breathing and the occasional scrape of her wings against the surrounding metal. The air grew marginally fresher as she climbed, suggesting proximity to the surface and fuelling her determination.

Finally, after what felt like an eternity suspended in vertical purgatory, her outstretched hand met the solid surface of a ceiling hatch. Pushing upward with all her strength, muscles straining with the effort, she lifted the hatch just enough to create a narrow slit through which to peer. Her eyes, adjusted to the darkness, were momentarily dazzled by the comparatively bright light filtering through. Blinking away the discomfort, she confirmed she was now exactly where she needed to be: the entry point to the vampire quarters where she hoped to intercept Warden Isolde.

Lilyana listened intently for any sign of movement, straining to detect footsteps, voices, or the rustle of fabric that might betray the presence of guards. Hearing nothing to indicate immediate danger, she pushed the hatch fully open with a final surge of strength and pulled herself up into the corridor, her muscles throbbing with the exertion. Her legs trembled visibly as she stood upright for the first time in what felt like forever, partly from the strain and partly from the overwhelming realisation that she had made it this far.

The reprieve was momentary. Lilyana froze as her sharp eyes caught movement. Just as she had hoped – yet still startling in its perfect timing – the unmistakable figure of Warden Isolde emerged from a doorway about fifteen paces ahead. The warden carried a clipboard in one pale hand, her attention fixed on the reports she was reviewing as she walked. Around her throat, gleaming tantalisingly even in the subdued lighting, hung the golden key – Lilyana's elusive chance at freedom.

Lilyana pressed herself flat against the wall in a shadowed recess between two decorative columns, willing herself to become one with the darkness. Her heart hammered so violently in her chest she feared it might give her away. Warden Isolde hadn't seen her yet – she was entirely focused on whatever administrative details demanded her attention as she walked with purposeful strides. But she was heading directly towards Lilyana's position, the distance between them shrinking with each passing second.

Lilyana could feel it now – the subtle current of energy that had been blocked during her time in the prison underground, flowing through her once more as it had from the day she was born. Her magic, dormant but not forgotten, stirred within her like a waking creature stretching after a long hibernation, tingling through her veins with electric familiarity. Fae magic wasn't combat-orientated like vampire abilities; it was subtle, rooted in nature and transformation, connected to ancient rhythms that predated modern understanding. But it could be weaponised, especially against a vampire with a known weakness – a fact Lilyana had contemplated through countless sleepless nights.

As Warden Isolde approached, now just mere feet away, Lilyana made her decision. Closing her eyes briefly, she reached for her magic, envisioning the spell that had come to her during those long nights of planning when darkness and desperation had been her only companions. She felt the power respond, gathering at her fingertips with eager anticipation, cool and tingling like morning dew.

Stepping deliberately from the shadows just as Warden Isolde drew level with her position, Lilyana released the spell with a silent exhale.

A swarm of luminous blue butterflies erupted from her outstretched hands, their delicate wings beating in hypnotic unison, shedding a fine powder that sparkled in the dim corridor as they surrounded the startled warden. The vampire's eyes widened in shock, first at Lilyana's presence where no prisoner should be, then at the manifestation of magic she hadn't anticipated encountering in her own meticulously controlled domain.

"You..." she began, voice sharp with authority despite her surprise, reaching for the panic button on her polished leather belt.

But the butterfly spores had already taken effect, drifting through the air like glittering mist. Warden Isolde's eyes reddened instantly, the whites becoming inflamed as blood vessels dilated, her breath catching in a violent sneeze that echoed down the empty corridor. The clipboard clattered to the floor with a harsh sound that seemed to reverberate through the stillness as she raised both hands to her face, her normally composed features contorted in an allergic reaction far more severe than what Lilyana had witnessed during that fateful day in the laundry.

Not wasting a second of her precious advantage, Lilyana lunged forward, her body moving with newfound agility. She grasped the golden key that hung around Warden Isolde's neck, yanking it hard enough to break the chain. The metal felt cold against her palm. Warden Isolde reached for her, fangs bared despite her distress, her moonlight-pale fingers grasping at empty air as another wave of violent sneezes doubled her over, rendering her efforts useless.

Lilyana turned and ran down the corridor. The magic flowing through her felt euphoric after so long without it, like drinking water after days of thirst, strengthening her limbs and sharpening her senses until the dimly lit passage seemed bright as day.

Behind her, alarms began to sound with piercing urgency – Warden Isolde had managed to trigger the security system. The wailing sirens cut through the silence like knives, echoing off stone walls and sending vibrations through the floor. Lilyana's brief advantage was evaporating quickly.

Following the corridor to its end, heart pounding against her ribs like a caged bird, she found herself facing the very door her entire plan hinged on – the main security door to the vampire quarters proper, a towering slab of reinforced steel etched with intricate sigils that seemed to swirl and intertwine in decorative patterns, adding an air of ancient mystique to the otherwise imposing barrier.

Inserting the golden key with shaking hands, sweat beading on her brow despite the chill in the air, Lilyana turned it in the lock. For one heart-stopping moment as the mechanism resisted, she feared it wouldn't work – that she had stolen the wrong key or that the door required additional authentication, a potentially fatal flaw in her plan.

The lock yielded with a satisfying click, and Lilyana charged through the grand corridors of the vampire quarters, her footsteps muffled on the plush red carpet beneath her feet. It was the first time she had felt such luxury since her capture. The space was illuminated by elegant sconces, casting a warm, flickering glow over the opulent surroundings – dark mahogany panelling, rich velvet furniture in various shades of crimson, and towering portraits of ancient vampire nobility watching silently from the walls. The air was thick with the scent of expensive incense, an almost intoxicating contrast to the pungent prison below. Even in the midst of her frantic escape, she couldn't ignore the overwhelming grandeur.

She just needed to find one window – ideally already open to the world beyond – and then she would be free of this prison.

Chapter Nine

Wind swept through Lilyana's hair as she soared through the early evening sky. The crisp air against her face felt like the purest form of liberation after the stale confines of the prison. Below her, Grindmore Prison Academy receded into the distance. She had found an unlatched window on the upper floor of the vampire quarters, slipped through it like a whisper, and launched herself into the world beyond.

As she curved her wings to catch a thermal, lifting her higher above the sprawling city of Grindmore, Lilyana's exhilaration was briefly interrupted by unbidden thoughts of those she'd left behind. As their faces flashed through her mind, a twist of guilt tightened in her stomach.

She shook her head fiercely, dispelling the thought. The prison reduced everyone to survival, stripped away any illusion of community or co-operation. Any one of them would have done exactly as she had – seized their chance when it came, regardless of who was left behind.

"They would have done the same," she whispered to the wind, the words immediately carried away by the rushing air. "They would have done exactly the same."

Flying low now, skimming just above the treetops to avoid being spotted against the darkening sky, Lilyana angled her wings towards the city's outskirts. Her muscles ached from the exertion after months of disuse, but the pain felt glorious – a tangible reminder of her escape. She knew the vampires would already be searching for her, their network of informants spread throughout the city. Grindmore was no longer safe for her, and soon it would not be safe for those she loved.

Her family's small cottage came into view, nestled among a cluster of similar dwellings at the edge of the fae district. Smoke curled from the chimney in lazy spirals, and warm light spilled from the windows into the gathering dusk. The sight brought a lump to her throat. Home. But she couldn't stay – none of them could.

Lilyana descended in a tight spiral, landing in the small garden behind the cottage. Her legs trembled slightly as she folded her wings, the pink membrane glimmering in the fading light. Taking a deep breath to steady herself, she approached the back door and pushed it open without knocking.

The familiar scents of home enveloped her – baking bread, dried herbs hanging from the rafters, and the distinctive floral perfume her mother always wore. The kitchen was warm and bright, so at odds with the cold sterility of the prison that tears sprang to Lilyana's eyes.

Her mother – Aralina – stood at the stove, her back turned as she stirred something in a large pot. Aralina was tall and willowy, her wings a deeper, more reddish pink than Lilyana's, folded neatly against her back. Her dark hair was swept up in a practical knot, streaked with premature silver that must have appeared following Lilyana's arrest. She hummed softly as she worked, unaware of her daughter's presence.

At the kitchen table sat Tarian, Lilyana's younger brother, hunched over a book, his brow furrowed in concentration. At fourteen, he was already showing signs of the height he would eventually achieve, all gangly limbs and awkward movements. His wings were a paler pink than either his mother's or sister's, almost translucent in the kitchen's warm light. His fingers, ink-stained from writing, tapped an absent rhythm on the tabletop as he read.

"Mother," Lilyana said, her voice breaking. "Tarian."

Both figures froze, then turned in perfect synchronicity. For a moment, no one moved or spoke, the only sound the gentle bubbling of whatever was cooking on the stove.

"Lily?" her mother whispered, the wooden spoon clattering to the floor. "Is it... is it really you?"

Tarian shot to his feet, knocking his chair over backward with a crash. "Lily!" he cried, his adolescent voice cracking with emotion.

Before Lilyana could respond, they were both rushing towards her, enveloping her in a tangle of arms and wings, their voices overlapping in a chorus of questions and exclamations. Her mother's hands frantically searched her face, as if to confirm she was real and not some cruel illusion, while Tarian clung to her with a strength that surprised her.

"How did you…"
"We thought you wouldn't be released for…"
"Are you alright? Have they hurt you?"
"Did they let you go? Are you…"

"Listen to me," Lilyana interrupted urgently, gently but firmly disentangling herself from their embrace. "There's no time to explain everything. We need to leave Grindmore. Tonight. Now."

Her mother's face paled, understanding dawning in her eyes. "You escaped," she said, not a question but a statement. "They'll be looking for you."

"They'll come here first," Lilyana confirmed. "We need to be gone before they arrive. All of us."

Tarian's eyes widened. "But... everything we have is here. My books, your crystals, Mother's garden..."

"None of that matters," Lilyana said, grasping his shoulders. "We need to get out of here."

"But where will we go?" her mother asked, already moving with purpose, gathering a few essential items from around the kitchen. "What will we do?"

"Mystvale," Lilyana said without hesitation. "The next city over. It's beyond vampire jurisdiction. We can start again there." She glanced out the window anxiously. "We need to hurry. Don't pack much – just what you can carry without slowing us down."

Her mother nodded grimly. "Five minutes," she said. "Tarian, get your warmest cloak and a change of clothes. Nothing more."

As her family scrambled to gather the bare essentials, Lilyana stood guard by the window, scanning the darkening street for any sign of vampire patrols. Her heart hammered in her chest, each passing minute stretching her nerves tighter.

True to her word, Aralina reappeared in exactly five minutes, a small pack slung over her shoulder. Tarian followed close behind, clutching a battered satchel to his chest, his young face set in determined lines that made him look suddenly older.

"We're ready," Aralina said simply.

Lilyana nodded, fighting back tears. "The eastern border is least patrolled. We'll head that way on foot – flying would make us too visible."

They slipped out through the back door, leaving the pot still bubbling on the stove and lights still burning in the windows – a home abandoned in haste, with no proper farewell. The thought tightened Lilyana's throat, but she pushed the sentiment aside. Sentimentality was a luxury they couldn't afford.

Moving through the shadows, the three fae made their way through the outskirts of Grindmore. They stuck to narrow alleyways and overgrown paths, avoiding the main thoroughfares where vampire patrols would be most likely. Occasionally, they would freeze at the sound of footsteps or voices, pressing themselves into doorways or behind trees until the danger had passed.

Tarian stumbled once, fatigue and fear making him clumsy, and Lilyana caught him before he fell, her reflexes honed by months of vigilance in the prison. The brief gratitude in his eyes nearly undid her composure.

"We're almost there," she whispered, as much to reassure herself as to reassure him.

The border of Grindmore was indicated by nothing more than a simple stone marker – the vampires had never seen the need for walls or checkpoints to keep people in. Most fae remained in the city simply because it was all they had ever known, their lives and livelihoods bound to a place that treated them as second-class citizens but was nevertheless home. The true barriers were invisible ones – fear, complacency, and the ties of community that made the prospect of leaving seem more daunting than staying.

Lilyana paused at the marker, her family beside her. Behind them lay the only home they had ever known; ahead, uncertainty but also possibility. She thought of the prison, of Warden Isolde, of the countless fae still trapped within those walls. For a moment, doubt clouded her resolve.

"Are we doing the right thing?" Tarian asked in a small voice, echoing her unspoken question.

"Yes," she said firmly. "At least out there, we have a chance."

Her mother reached out, taking both their hands in hers. As one, the three fae stepped across the border, leaving Grindmore behind. The physical sensation was unremarkable – simply one foot in front of the other – but Lilyana felt the symbolic enormity of the moment.

They did not look back as they set off along the road to Mystvale, their shadows stretching in the light of the rising moon. The path ahead was long and uncertain, their future unwritten. But for the first time since her arrest, Lilyana felt something unfamiliar yet unmistakable unfurling in her chest: hope – not the desperate kind, but something pure, steady, and undeterred.

Epilogue

Morning sunlight streamed through open windows, casting golden patterns across the wooden floor of a modest but comfortable workshop. Lilyana's fingers wove delicate strands of enchanted silk into an intricate design. Around her neck, the golden key from Grindmore Prison Academy hung on its repaired chain, catching the light as she bent over her work.

Three years had passed since that desperate escape from Grindmore. Mystvale had proven to be everything they had hoped for – a city where fae lived as equals, not as subjects to vampire rule. The transition had not been easy; they had arrived with almost nothing, forced to rebuild their lives from the ground up. But freedom, Lilyana had discovered, was fertile soil in which even the most tentative beginnings could flourish.

Her mother now ran a small but popular apothecary, her knowledge of healing in high demand among Mystvale's diverse population. Tarian had flourished in the city's academy, his natural intelligence finding expression in studies that would have been forbidden to him in Grindmore. Lilyana had discovered her own talent for weaving enchantments into textiles, creating garments and accessories that carried subtle magic within their threads.

She paused in her work, her fingers instinctively rising to touch the key on the chain around her neck. It had become an unconscious habit – a touchstone that grounded her whenever memories of the prison threatened to resurface. She wore it always: a reminder of the value of freedom, a symbol of her courage, and a keepsake – just in case it would prove useful again.

Sometimes, in quiet moments like this, Lilyana found herself thinking about the fae she had left behind. Had any of them found their way to freedom? Or did they remain trapped within those subterranean walls, counting days that blurred into months and years?

She had never fully trusted any of them – couldn't afford to in a place where survival often meant looking out for oneself above all others. Yet something in her had changed since escaping. Perhaps it was the security of her new life, or the perspective that came with time and distance, but she found herself hoping that somehow, they too had found their way out.

"One day," she whispered to the key, as she sometimes did when alone, "they'll all be free."

She didn't know how such freedom might come – whether through individual escapes like her own, or some larger change that would topple the vampire regime entirely. The vampires had ruled for generations, and their power seemed unshakable. Yet Lilyana clung to the hope that it wouldn't last forever. She had exploited a weakness in one of them, and if she could do it, there was every possibility that others could too. If enough fae could rise and strike back, there might one day come a time when none would have to live in fear again.

Until then, Lilyana would live the freedom she had claimed – not just for herself, but for all of them. The future was uncertain, but as long as the hope of resistance burned, she knew the fight was far from over.